To Sam, my stargazer
—A.B.

For Katie, who sees more than others do,
even with her eyes closed
—S.J. and L.F.

Text copyright © 2013 by Ann Bonwill
Jacket art and interior illustrations copyright © 2013 by Steve Johnson and Lou Fancher

All rights reserved. Published in the United States by Random House Children's Books, a division of Random House, Inc., New York.

Random House and the colophon are registered trademarks of Random House, Inc.

Visit us on the Web! randomhouse.com/kids

Educators and librarians, for a variety of teaching tools, visit us at RHTeachersLibrarians.com

Library of Congress Cataloging-in-Publication Data
Bonwill, Ann.
When mermaids sleep / by Ann Bonwill ; illustrated by Steven Johnson & Lou Fancher.
p. cm.
Summary: When the moon shines into your room at night and casts a dreamy light, it is time to say good night.
ISBN 978-0-375-87061-3 (trade) — ISBN 978-0-375-97061-0 (lib. bdg.)
[1. Stories in rhyme. 2. Bedtime—Fiction.] I. Johnson, Steve, 1960–, ill. II. Fancher, Lou, ill. III. Title.
PZ8.3.B6442Whe 2013 [E]—dc23 2012001881

MANUFACTURED IN CHINA

10 9 8 7 6 5 4 3 2 1

First Edition

WHEN MERMAIDS SLEEP

By Ann Bonwill

Illustrated by Steve Johnson & Lou Fancher

RANDOM HOUSE 🏠 NEW YORK

When mermaids sleep in oceans deep
inside their coral caves,
they lay their heads on seaweed beds,
rocked softly by the waves.

Those same waves carry sailing ships
from shore to distant shore.
Abed in bunks, asleep on trunks,
the scruffy pirates snore.

Inside those rusty iron trunks
their stolen treasures gleam,
dug up from sands in far-off lands
where genies gently dream.

That same sand builds a castle strong
with towers ten in number,
where all afloat, within the moat,
the royal serpents slumber.

Atop those towers in the sky
the regal wizards keep
their eyes on Mars and all the stars
before they fall asleep.

Those same stars twinkle in the woods
where ivy hangs like eaves
and unicorns rest tired horns
on pillows made of leaves.

On wings of wind those leaves are swept
to mighty mountains high,
where tall crests shake and valleys quake
as sleeping giants sigh.

In those same valleys, blue with dusk,
inside the giants' shoes,
snuggled tight in blankets white,
the sneaky goblins snooze.

Those blankets white are made from snow,
whose lacy falling flakes
drift to the west, where griffins nest—
shh! now one awakes.

Far below those same large nests
in tunnels underground,
glowing bugs in round glass jugs
with dozing dwarves are found.

Those tunnels lead up through the earth.
They'll reach the surface soon,
where fairies lie on flowers high
and sleep beneath the moon.

Into your room shines that same moon
and casts a dreamy light.
Close your eyes as magic flies.
It's time to say . . .

. . . good night.